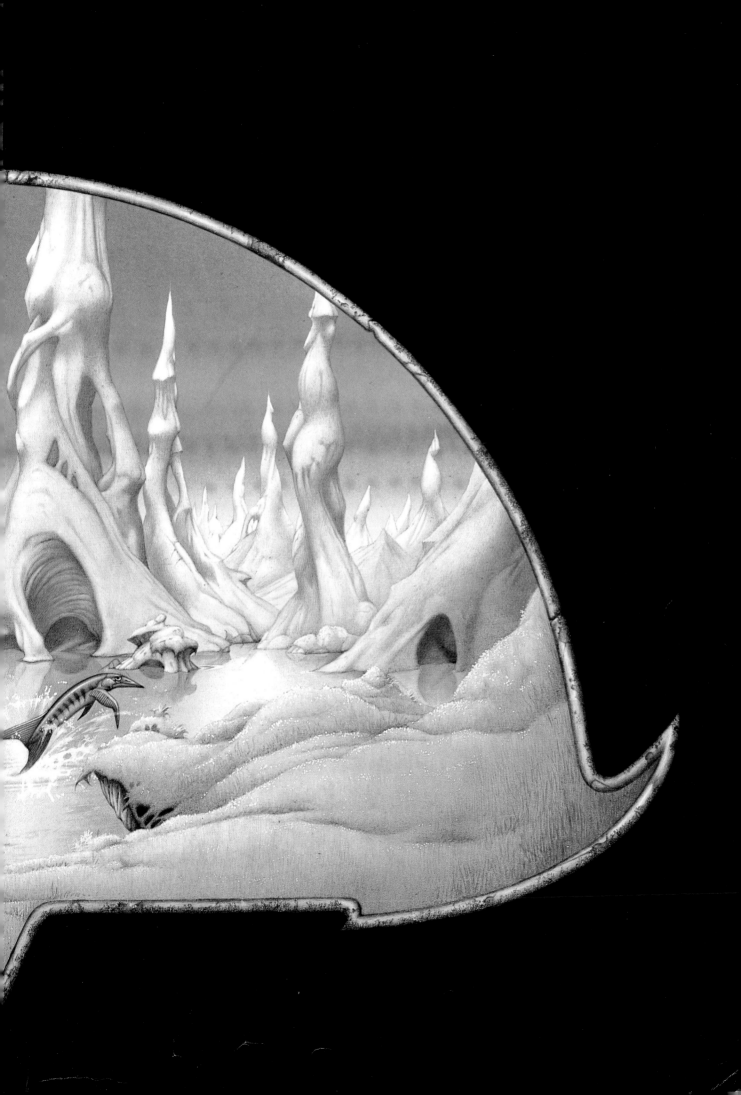

In Which Mrs Pearsson Detects An Above Average Degree of Chaos In The Megaflow

Returning from China to London and the Spring of 1936, Una Persson found an unfamiliar quality of pathos in most of the friends she had last seen, as far as she recalled, during the Blitz on her way back from 1970. Then they had been desperately hearty: it was a comfort to understand that the condition was not permanent. Here, at present, Pierrot ruled and she felt she possessed a better grip on her power. This was, she admitted with shame, her favourite moral climate for it encouraged in her an enormously gratifying sense of spiritual superiority: the advantage of having been born, originally, into a later and probably more sophisticated age. The 1960s. Some women, she reflected, were forced to have children in order to enjoy this pleasure.

But she was uneasy, so she reported to the local Time Centre and the bearded, sullen features of Sergeant Alvarez who welcomed her in white, apologizing for the fact that he had himself only just that morning left the Lower Devonian and had not had time to change.

'It's the megaflow, as you guessed,' he told her, operating toggles to reveal his crazy display systems. 'We've lost control.'

'We never really had it.' She lit a Sherman's and shook her long hair back over the headrest of the swivel chair, opening her military overcoat and loosening her webbing. 'Is it worse than usual?'

'Much.' He sipped cold coffee from his battered silver mug. 'It cuts through every plane we can pick up — a rogue current swerving through the dimensions. Something of a twister.'

'Jerry?'

'He's dormant. We checked. But it's like him, certainly. Most Probably another aspect.'

'Oh, sod.' Una straightened her shoulders.

'That's what I thought,' said Alvarez. 'Some-one's going to have to do a spot of rubato.' He studied a screen. It was Greek to Una. For a moment a pattern formed. Alvarez made a note. 'Yes. It can either be fixed at the nadir or the zenith. It's too late to try anywhere in between. I think it's up to you, Mrs P.'

She got to her feet. 'Where's the zenith?'

'The End of Time.'

'Well,' she said, 'that's something.'

She opened her bag and made sure of her jar of instant coffee. It was the one thing she couldn't get at the End of Time.

'Sorry,' said Alvarez, glad that the expert had been there and that he could remain behind.

'It's just as well,' she said. 'This period's no good for my moral well-being. I'll be off, then.'

'Someone's got to.' Alvarez failed to seem sympathetic.

'It's Chaos out there.'

'You don't have to tell me.'

She entered the make-shift chamber and was on her way to the End of Time.

2

In Which The Eternal Champion Finds Himself at the End of Time

Elric of Melniboné shook a bone-white fist at the greedy, glaring stars — the eyes of all those men whose souls he had stolen to sustain his own enfeebled body. He looked down. Though it seemed he stood on something solid, there was only more blackness falling away below him. It was as if he hung at the centre of the universe. And here, too, were staring points of yellow light. Was he to be judged?

His half-sentient runesword, Stormbringer, in its scabbard on his left hip, murmured like a nervous dog.

He had been on his way to Imrryr, to his home, to reclaim his kingdom from his cousin Yyrkoon; sailing from the Isle of the Purple Towns where he had guested with Count Smiorgan Baldhead. Magic winds had caught the Filkharian trader as she crossed the unnamed water between the Vilmirian peninsula and the Isle of Melniboné. She had been borne into the Dragon Sea and thence to The Sorcerer's Isle, so-called because that barren place had been the home of Cran Liret, the Thief of Spells, a wizard infamous for his borrowings, who had, at length, been dispatched by those he sought to rival. But much residual magic had been left behind. Certain spells had come into the keeping of the Krettii, a tribe of near-brutes who had migrated to the island from the region of The Silent Land less than fifty years before. Their shaman, one Grrodd Ybene Eenr, had made unthinking use of devices buried by the dying sorcerer as the spells of his peers sucked life and sanity from them. Elric had dealt with more than one clever wizard, but never with so mindless a power. His battle had been long and exhausting and had required the sacrifice of most of the Filkharians as well as the entire tribe of Krettii. His sorcery had become increasingly desperate. Sprite fought sprite, devil fell upon devil, in both physical and astral, all around the region of The Sorcerer's Isle. Eventually Elric had mounted a massive summoning against the allies of Grrodd Ybene

Eenr with the result that the shaman had been at last overwhelmed and his remains scattered in Limbo. But Elric, captured by his own monstrous magickings, had followed his enemy and now he stood in the Void, crying out into appalling silence, hearing his words only in his skull:

'Arioch! Arioch! Aid me!'

But his patron Duke of Hell was absent. He could not exist here. He could not, for once, even hear his favourite protégé.

'Arioch! Repay my loyalty! I have given you blood and souls!'

He did not breathe. His heart had stopped. All his movements were sluggish.

The eyes looked down at him. They looked up at him. Were they glad? Did they rejoice in his terror?

'Arioch!'

He yearned for a reply. He would have wept, but no tears would come. His body was cold; less than dead, yet not alive. A fear was in him greater than any fear he had known before.

'Oh, Arioch! Aid me!'

He forced his right hand towards the pulsing pommel of Stormbringer which, alone, still possessed energy. The hilt of the sword was warm to his touch and, as slowly he folded his fingers around it, it seemed to swell in his fist and propel his arm upwards so that he did not draw the sword. Rather the sword forced his limbs into motion.

And now it challenged the void, glowing with black fire, singing its high, gleeful battlesong.

'Our destinies are intertwined, Stormbringer,' said Elric. 'Bring us from this place, or those destinies shall never be fulfilled.'

Stormbringer swung like the needle of a compass and Elric's unfeeling arm was wrenched round to go with it. In eight directions the sword swung, as if to the eight points of Chaos. It was questing — like a hound sniffing a trail. Then a yell sounded from within the strange metal of the blade; a distant cry of delight, it seemed to Elric. The sound one would hear if one stood above a valley listening to children playing far below.

Elric knew that Stormbringer had sensed a plane they might reach. Not necessarily their

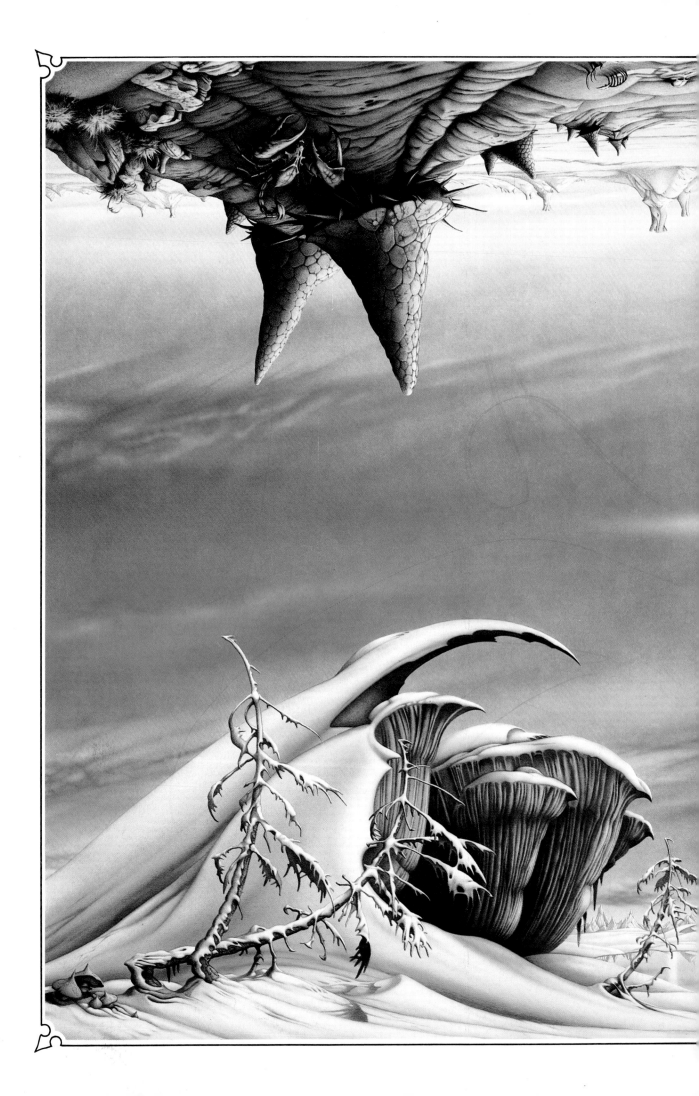

own, but one which would accept them. And, as a drowning mariner must yearn for the most inhospitable rock rather than no rock at all, Elric yearned for that plane.

'*Stormbringer. Take us there!*'

The sword hesitated. It moaned. It was suspicious.

'*Take us there!*' whispered the albino to his runesword.

The sword struck back and forth, up and down, as if it battled invisible enemies. Elric scarcely kept his grip on it. It seemed that Stormbringer was frightened of the world it had detected and sought to drive it back but the act of seeking had in itself set them both in motion. Already Elric could feel himself being drawn through the darkness, towards something he could see very dimly beyond the myriad eyes, as dawn reveals clouds undetected in the night sky.

Elric thought he saw the shapes of crags, pointed and crazy. He thought he saw water, flat and ice-blue. The stars faded and there was snow beneath his feet, mountains all around him, a huge, blazing sun overhead — and above that another landscape, a desert, as a magic mirror might reflect the contrasting character of he who peered into it — a desert, quite as real as the snowy peaks in which he crouched, sword in hand, waiting for one of these landscapes to fade so that he might establish, to a degree, his bearings. Evidently the two planes had intersected.

But the landscape overhead did not fade. He could look up and see sand, mountains, vegetation, a sky which met his own sky at a point half-way along the curve of the huge sun — and blended with it. He looked about him. Snowy peaks in all directions. Above — desert everywhere. He felt dizzy, found that he was staring downwards, reaching to cup some of the snow in his hand. It was ordinary snow, though it seemed reluctant to melt in contact with his flesh.

'This is a world of Chaos,' he muttered. 'It obeys no natural laws.' His voice seemed loud, amplified by the peaks, perhaps. 'That is why you did not want to come here. This is the world of powerful rivals.'

Stormbringer was silent, as if all its energy

were spent. But Elric did not sheath the blade. He began to trudge through the snow towards what seemed to be an abyss. Every so often he glanced upward, but the desert overhead had not faded, sun and sky remained the same. He wondered if he walked around the surface of a miniature world. That if he continued to go forward he might eventually reach the point where the two landscapes met. He wondered if this were not some punishment wished upon him by his untrustworthy allies of Chaos. Perhaps he must choose between death in the snow or death in the desert. He reached the edge of the abyss and looked down.

The walls of the abyss fell for all of five feet before reaching a floor of gold and siver squares which stretched for perhaps another seven feet before they reached the far wall, where the landscape continued — snow and crags — uninterrupted.

'This is undoubtedly where Chaos rules,' said the Prince of Melniboné. He studied the smooth, chequered floor. It reflected parts of the snowy terrain and the desert world above it. It reflected the crimson-eyed albino who

peered down at it, his features drawn in bewilderment and tiredness.

'I am at their mercy,' said Elric. 'They play with me. But I shall resist them, even as they destroy me.' And some of his wild, careless spirit came back to him as he prepared to lower himself onto the chequered floor and cross to the opposite bank.

He was half-way over when he heard a grunting sound in the distance and a beast appeared, its paws slithering uncertainly on the smooth surface, its seven savage eyes glaring in all directions as if it sought the instigator of its terrible indignity.

And, at last, all seven eyes focused on Elric and the beast opened a mouth in which row upon row of thin, vicious teeth were arranged, and uttered a growl of unmistakable resentment.

Elric raised his sword. 'Back creature of Chaos. You threaten the Prince of Melniboné!'

The beast was already propelling itself towards him. Elric flung his body to one side, aiming a blow with the sword as he did so, succeeding only in making a thin incision in the monster's heavily muscled hind leg. It shrieked and began to turn.

'Back!'

Elric's voice was the brave, thin squeak of a lemming attacked by a hawk. He drove at the thing's snout with Stormbringer. The sword was heavy. It had spent all its energy and there was no more to give. Elric wondered why he, himself, did not weaken. Possibly the laws of nature were entirely abolished in the Realm of Chaos. He struck and drew blood. The beast paused, more in astonishment than fear.

Then it opened its jaws, pushed its back legs against the snowy bank, and shot towards the albino who tried to dodge it, lost his footing, and fell, sprawling backwards, on the gold and silver surface.

In Which Una Persson Discovers An Unexpected Snag

The gigantic beetle, rainbow carapace glittering, turned as if into the wind, which blew from the distant mountains, its thick, flashing wings beating rapidly as it bore its single passenger over the queer landscape.

On its back Mrs Persson checked the instruments on her wrist. Ever since Man had begun to travel in time it had become necessary for the League to develop techniques to compensate for the fluctuations and disruptions in the space-time continua; perpetually monitoring the chronoflow and megaflow. She pursed her lips. She had picked up the signal. She made the semi-sentient beetle swing a degree or two SSE and head directly for the mountains. She was in some sort of enclosed (but vast) environment. These mountains, as well as everything surrounding them, lay in the territory must utilized by the gloomy, naturalborn Werther de Goethe, poet and romantic, solitary seeker after truth in a world no longer differentiating between the degrees of reality. He would not remember her, she knew, because, as far as Werther was concerned, they had not met yet. He had not even, if Una were correct, experienced his adventure with Mistress Christia, the Everlasting Concubine. A story on which she had dined out more than once, in duller eras.

The mountains drew closer. From here it was possible to see the entire arrangement (a creation of Werther's very much in character): a desert landscape, a central sun, and, inverted above it, winter mountains. Werther strove to make statements, like so many naïve artists before him, by presenting simple contrasts: The World is Bleak/The World is Cold/Barren Am I As I Grow Old/Tomorrow I Die, Entombed in Cold/For Silver My Poor Soul Was Sold — she remembered he was perhaps the worst poet she had encountered in an eternity of meetings with bad poets. He had taught himself to read and write in old, old English so that he might carve those words on one of his many abandoned tombs (half his time was spent in composing obituaries for himself). Like so many others he seemed to

equate self-pity with artistic inspiration. In an earlier age he might have discovered his public and become quite rich (self-pity passing for passion in the popular understanding). Sometimes she regretted the passing of Wheldrake, so long ago, so far away, in a universe bearing scarcely any resemblances to those in which she normally operated.

She brought her wavering mind back to the problem. The beetle dipped and circled over the desert, but there was no sight of her quarry.

She was about to abandon the search when she heard a faint roaring overhead and she looked up to see another characteristic motif of Werther's — a gold and silver chessboard on which, upside down, a monstrous dog-like creature was bearing down on a tiny white-haired man dressed in the most abominable taste Una had seen for some time.

She directed the aircar upwards and then, reversing the machine as she entered the opposing gravity, downwards to where the barbarically costumed swordsman was about to be eaten by the beast.

'Shoo!' cried Una commandingly.

The beast raised a befuddled head.

'Shoo.'

It licked its lips and returned its seven-eyed gaze to the albino, who was now on his knees, using his large sword to steady himself as he climbed to his feet.

The jaws opened wider and wider. The pale man prepared, shakily, to defend himself.

Una directed the aircar at the beast's unkempt head. The great beetle connected with a loud crack. The monster's eyes widened in dismay. It yelped. It sat on its haunches and began to slide away, its claws making an unpleasant noise on the gold and silver tiles.

Una landed the aircar and gestured for the stranger to enter. She noticed with distaste that he was a somewhat unhealthy looking albino with gaunt features, exaggeratedly large and slanting eyes, ears that were virtually pointed, and glaring, half-mad red pupils.

And yet, undoubtedly, it was her quarry and there was nothing for it but to be polite.

'Do, please, get in,' she said. 'I am here to rescue you.'

'Shaarmraaam torjistoo quellahm vyeearrr,'

said the stranger in an accent that seemed to Una to be vaguely Scottish.

'Damn,' she said, 'that's all we need.' She had been anxious to approach the albino in private, before one of the denizens of the End of Time could arrive and select him for a menagerie, but now she regretted that Werther or perhaps Lord Jagged were not here, for she realized that she needed one of their translation pills, those tiny tablets which could 'engineer' the brain to understand a new language. By a fluke — or perhaps because of her presence here so often — the people at the End of Time currently spoke formal early twentieth-century English.

The albino — who wore a kind of tartan divided kilt, knee-length boots, a blue and white jerkin, a green cloak and a silver breastplate, with a variety of leather belts and metal buckles here and there upon his person — was vehemently refusing her offer of a lift. He raised the sword before him as he backed away, slipped once, reached the bank, scrambled through snow and disappeared behind a rock.

Mrs Persson sighed and put the car into motion again.

'4'

In Which The Prince of Melniboné Encounters Further Terrors

Xiombarg herself, thought Elric as he slid beneath the snows into the cave. Well, he would have no dealings with the Queen of Chaos; not until he was forced to do so.

The cave was large. In the thin light from the gap above his head he could not see far. He wondered whether to return to the surface or risk going deeper into the cave. There was always the hope that he would find another way out. He was attempting to recall some rune that would aid him, but all he knew depended either upon the aid of elementals who did not exist on this plane, or upon the Lords of Chaos themselves — and they were unlikely to come to his assistance in their own Realm. He was marooned here: the single mouse in a world of cats.

Almost unconsciously he found himself moving downwards, realizing that the cave had become a tunnel. He was feeling hungry but, apart from the monster and the woman in

the magical carriage, had seen no sign of life. Even the cavern did not seem entirely natural.

It widened; there was phosphorescent light. He realized that the walls were of transparent crystal and, behind the walls, were all manner of artefacts. He saw crowns, sceptres and chains of precious jewels; cabinets of complicated carving; weapons of strangely turned metal; armour, clothing, things whose use he could not guess — and food. There were sweetmeats, fruits, flans and pies, all out of reach.

Elric groaned. This was torment. Perhaps deliberately planned torment. A thousand voices whispered to him in a beautiful, alien language:

'*Bie-meee ... Bie-meee ...*' the voices murmured. '*Baa-gen-baa-gen ...*'

They seemed to be promising every delight, if only he could pass through the walls; but they were of transparent quartz, lit from within. He raised Stormbringer, half-tempted to try to break down the barrier, but he knew that even his sword was, at its most powerful, incapable of destroying the magic of Chaos.

He paused, gasping with astonishment at a group of small dogs which looked at him with large brown eyes, tongues lolling, and jumped up at him.

'*O, Nee Tubbens!*' intoned one of the voices.

'Gods!' screamed Elric. 'This torture is too much!' He swung his body this way and that, threatening with his sword, but the voices continued to murmur and promise, displaying their riches but never allowing him to touch.

The albino panted. His crimson eyes glared about him. 'You would drive me insane, eh? Well, Elric of Melniboné has witnessed more frightful threats than this. You will need to do more if you would destroy his mind!'

And he ran through the whispering passages, looking to neither his right nor his left, until, quite suddenly, he had run into blazing daylight and stood staring down into pale infinity — a blue and endless void.

He looked up. And he screamed.

Overhead were the gentle hills and dales of a rural landscape, with rivers, grazing cattle, woods and cottages. He expected to fall, headlong, but he did not. He was on the brink of the abyss. The cliff-face of red sandstone fell immediately below and then was the tranquil void. He looked back:

'Baa-gen ... O, Nee Tubbens ...'

A bitter smile played about the albino's bloodless lips as, decisively, he sheathed his sword.

'Well, then,' he said. 'Let them do their worst!'

And, laughing, he launched himself over the brink of the cliff.

'5'

In Which Werther de Goethe Makes A Wonderful Discovery

With a gesture of quiet pride, Werther de Goethe indicated his gigantic skull.

'It is very large, Werther,' said Mistress Christia, the Everlasting Concubine, turning a power ring to adjust the shade of her eyes so that they perfectly matched the day.

'It is monstrous,' said Werther modestly. 'It reminds us all of the Inevitable Night.'

'Who was that?' enquired golden-haired Gaf the Horse in Tears, at present studying ancient legendry. 'Sir Lew Grady?'

'I mean Death,' Werther told him, 'which overwhelms us all.'

'Well, not us,' pointed out the Duke of Queens, as usual a trifle literal minded. 'Because we're immortal, as you know.'

Werther offered him a sad, pitying look and sighed briefly. 'Retain your delusions, if you will.'

Mistress Christia stroked the gloomy Werther's long, dark locks. 'There, there,' she said. 'We have compensations, Werther.'

'Without Death,' intoned the Last Romantic, 'there is no point to Life.'

As usual, they could not follow him, but they nodded gravely and politely.

'The skull,' continued Werther, stroking the side of his aircar (which was in the shape of a large flying reptile) to make it circle and head for the left eye-socket, 'is a Symbol not only of our Morality, but also of our Fruitless Ambitions.'

'Fruit?' Bishop Castle, drowsing at the rear of the vehicle, became interested. His hobby was currently orchards. 'Less? My pine-trees, you know, are proving a problem. The apples are much smaller than I was led to believe.'

'The skull is lovely, said Mistress Christia with valiant enthusiasm. 'Well, now that we have seen it . . .'

'The outward shell,' Werther told her. 'It is what it hides which is more important. Man's Foolish Yearnings are all encompassed therein. His Greed, his Need for the Impossible, the Heat of his Passions, the Coldness which must Finally Overtake him. Through this eye-socket you will encounter a little invention of my own called The Bargain Basement of the Mind ...'

He broke off in astonishment.

On the top edge of the eye-socket a tiny figure had emerged.

'What's that?' enquired the Duke of Queens, craning his head back. 'A random thought?'

'It is not mine at all!'

The figure launched itself into the sky and seemed to fly, with flailing limbs, towards the sun.

Werther frowned, watching the tiny man disappear. 'The gravity field is reversed there,' he said absently, 'in order to make the most of the paradox, you understand. There is a snowscape, a desert ...' But he was much more interested in the newcomer. 'How do you think he got into my skull?'

'At least he's enjoying himself. He seems to be laughing.' Mistress Christia bent an ear towards the thin sound, which grew fainter and fainter at first, but became louder again. 'He's coming back.'

Werther nodded. 'Yes. The field's no longer reversed.' He touched a power ring.

The laughter stopped and became a yell of rage. The figure hurtled down on them. It had a sword in one white hand and its red eyes blazed.

Hastily, Werther stroked another ring. The stranger tumbled into the bottom of the aircar and lay there panting, cursing and groaning.

'How wonderful!' cried Werther. 'Oh, this is a traveller from some rich, romantic past. Look at him! What else could he be? What a prize!'

The stranger rose to his feet and raised the sword high above his head, defying the amazed and delighted passengers as he screamed at the top of his voice:
'Heegeegrowinaz!'

'Good afternoon,' said Mistress Christia. She reached in her purse for a translation pill and found one. 'I wonder if you would care to swallow this — it's quite harmless . . .'

The Duke of Queens pointed towards the other socket. A huge, whirring beetle came sailing from it. In its back was someone he recognized with pleasure. 'Mrs Persson!'

Una brought her aircar alongside.

'Is he in your charge?' asked Werther with

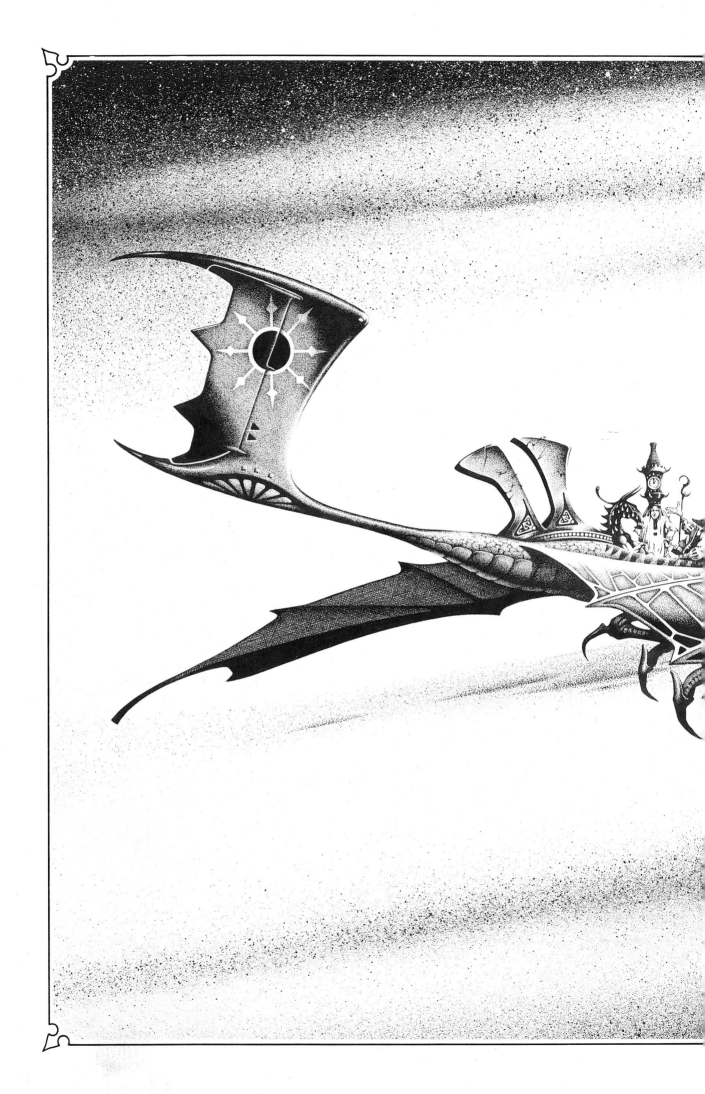

undisguised disappointment. 'If so, I could offer you ...'

'I'm afraid he means a lot to me,' she said.

'From you own age?' Mistress Christia also recognized Una. She still offered the translation pill in the palm of her hand. 'He seems a mite suspicious of us.'

'I'd noticed,' said Una. 'It would be useful if he would accept the pill. However, if he will not, one of us ...'

'I would be happy,' offered the generous Duke of Queens. He tugged at his green and gold beard. 'Werther de Goethe, Mrs Persson.'

'Perhaps I had better,' said Una nodding to Werther. The only problem with translation pills was that they did their job so thoroughly. You could speak the language perfectly, but you could speak no other.

Werther was, for once, positive. 'Let's all take a pill,' he suggested.

Everyone at the End of Time carried translation pills, in case of meeting a visitor from Space or the Past.

Mistress Christia handed hers to Una and found another. They swallowed.

'Creatures of Chaos,' said the newcomer with cool dignity, 'I demand that you release me. You cannot hold a mortal in this way, not unless he has struck a bargain with you. And no bargain was struck which would bring me to the Realm of Chaos.'

'It's actually more orderly than you'd think,' said Werther apologetically. 'Your first experience, you see, was the world of my skull, which was deliberately muddled. I meant to show what Confusion was the Mind of Man ...'

'May I introduce Mistress Christia, the Everlasting Concubine,' said the Duke of Queens, on his best manners. 'This is Mrs Persson, Bishop Castle, Gaf the Horse in Tears. Werther de Goethe — your unwitting host — and I am the Duke of Queens. We welcome you to our world. Your name, sir ...?'

'You must know me, my lord duke,' said Elric. 'For I am Elric of Melniboné, Emperor by Right of Birth, Inheritor of the Ruby Throne, Bearer of the Actorios, Wielder of the Black Sword ...'

'Indeed!' said Werther de Goethe. In a

whispered aside to Mrs Persson: 'What a marvellous scowl! What a noble sneer!'

'You are an important personage in your world, then?' said Mistress Christia, fluttering the eyelashes she had just extended by half an inch. 'Perhaps you would allow me ...'

'I think he wishes to be returned to his home,' said Mrs Persson hastily.

'Returned?' Werther was astonished. 'But the Morphail Effect! It is impossible.'

'Not in this case, I think,' she said. 'For if he is not returned there is no telling the fluctuations which will take place throughout the dimensions ...'

They could not follow her, but they accepted her tone.

'Aye,' said Elric darkly, 'return me to my realm, so that I may fulfil my own doom-laden destiny ...'

Werther looked upon the albino with affectionate delight. 'Aha! A fellow spirit! I, too, have a doom-laden destiny.'

'I doubt it is as doom-laden as mine.' Elric peered moodily back at the skull as the two aircars fled away towards a gentle horizon where exotic trees bloomed.

'Well,' said Werther with an effort, 'perhaps it is not, though I assure you ...'

'I have looked upon hell-born horror,' said Elric, 'and communicated with the very Gods of the Uttermost Darkness. I have seen things which would turn other men's minds to useless jelly ...'

'Jelly?' interrupted Bishop Castle. 'Do you, in your turn, have any expertise with, for instance, blackbird trees?'

'Your words are meaningless,' Elric told him, glowering. 'Why do you torment me so, my lords? I did not ask to visit your world. I belong in the world of men, in the Young Kingdoms, where I seek my weird. Why, I have but lately experienced adventures ...'

'I do think we have one of those bores,' murmured Bishop Castle to the Duke of Queens, 'so common amongst time-travellers. They all believe themselves unique.'

But the Duke of Queens refused to be drawn. He had developed a liking for the frowning albino. Gaf the Horse in Tears was also plainly impressed, for he had fashioned

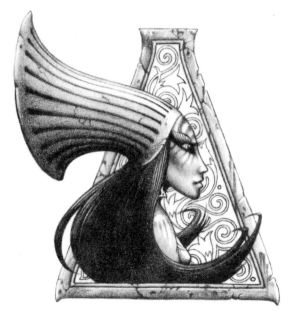

his own features into a rough likeness of Elric's. The Prince of Melniboné pretended insouciance, but it was evident to Una that he was frightened. She tried to calm him.

'People here at the End of Time ...' she began.

'No soft words, my lady.' A cynical smile played about the albino's lips. 'I know you for that great unholy temptress, Queen of the Swords, Xiombarg herself.'

'I assure you, I am as human as you, sir ...'

'Human? I, human? I am not human, madam — though I be a mortal, 'tis true. I am of older blood, the blood of the Bright Empire itself, the blood of R'lin K'ren A'a which Cran Liret mocked, not understanding what it was he laughed at. Aye, though forced to summon aid from Chaos, I made no bargain to become a slave in your realm ...'

'I assure you — um — your majesty,' said Una, 'that we had not meant to insult you and your presence here was no doing of ours. I am, as it happens, a stranger here myself. I came especially to see you, to help you escape ...'

'Ha! said the albino. 'I have heard such words before. You would lure me into some worse trap than this. Tell me, where is Duke Arioch? He, at least, I owe some allegiance to.'

'We have no one of that name,' apologized Mistress Christia. She enquired of Gaf, who knew everyone. 'No time-traveller?'

'None,' Gaf studied Elric's eyes and made a small adjustment to his own. He sat back, satisfied.

Elric shuddered and turned away mumbling.

'You are very welcome here,' said Werther. 'I cannot tell you how glad I am to meet one as essentially morbid and self-pitying as myself!'

Elric did not seem flattered.

'What can we do to make you feel at home?'

asked Mistress Christia. She had changed her hair to a rather glossy blue in the hope, perhaps, that Elric would find it more attractive. 'Is there anything you need?'

'Need? Aye. Peace of mind. Knowledge of my true destiny. A quiet place where I can be with Cymoril, whom I love.'

'What does this Cymoril look like?' Mistress Christia became just a trifle over-eager.

'She is the most beautiful creature in the universe,' said Elric.

'It isn't very much to go on,' said Mistress Christia. 'If you could imagine a picture, perhaps? There are devices in the old cities which could visualize your thoughts. We could go there. I should be happy to fill in for her, as it were ...'

'What? You offer me a simulacrum? Do you not think I should detect such witchery at once? Ah, this is loathsome! Slay me, if you will, or continue the torment. I'll listen no longer!'

They were floating now, between high cliffs. On a ledge far below a group of time-travellers pointed up at them. One waved desperately.

'You've offended him, Mistress Christia,'

said Werther pettishly. 'You don't understand how sensitive he is.'

'Yes I do.' She was aggrieved. 'I was only being sympathetic.'

'Sympathy!' Elric rubbed at his long, somewhat pointed jaw. 'Ha! What do I want with sympathy?'

'I never heard anyone who wanted it more.' Mistress Christia was kind. 'You're like a little boy, really, aren't you?'

'Compared to the ancient Lords of Chaos, I am a child, aye. But my blood is old and cold, the blood of decaying Meniboné, as well you know.' And with a huge sigh the albino seated himself at the far end of the car and rested his head on his fist. 'Well? What is your pleasure, my lords and ladies of Hell?'

'It is your pleasure we are anxious to achieve,' Werther told him. 'Is there anything at all we can do? Some environment we can manufacture? What are you used to?'

'Used to? I am used to the crack of leathery dragon wings in the sweet, sharp air of the early dawn. I am used to the sound of red battle, the drumming of hooves on bloody earth, the screams of the dying, the yells of the victorious. I am used to warring against demons and monsters, sorcerers and ghouls. I have sailed on magic ships and fought hand to hand with reptilian savages. I have encountered the Jade Man himself. I have fought side by side with the elementals, who are my allies. I have battled black evil ...'

'Well' said Werther, 'that's something to go on, at any rate. I'm sure we can ...'

'Lord Elric won't be staying,' began Una Persson politely. 'You see — these fluctuations in the megaflow — not to mention his own destiny ... He should not be here, at all, Werther.'

'Nonsense!' Werther flung a black velvet arm about the stiff shoulders of his new friend. 'It is evident that our destinies are one. Lord Elric is as grief-haunted as myself!' 'How can you know what it is to be haunted by grief?' murmured the albino. His face was half-buried in Werther's generous sleeve.

Mrs Persson controlled herself. She rose from Werther's aircar and made for her own. 'Well,' she said, 'I must be off. I hope to see you later, everybody.'

They sang out their farewells.

Una Persson turned her beetle westward, towards Castle Canaria, the home of her old friend Lord Jagged.

She needed help and advice.

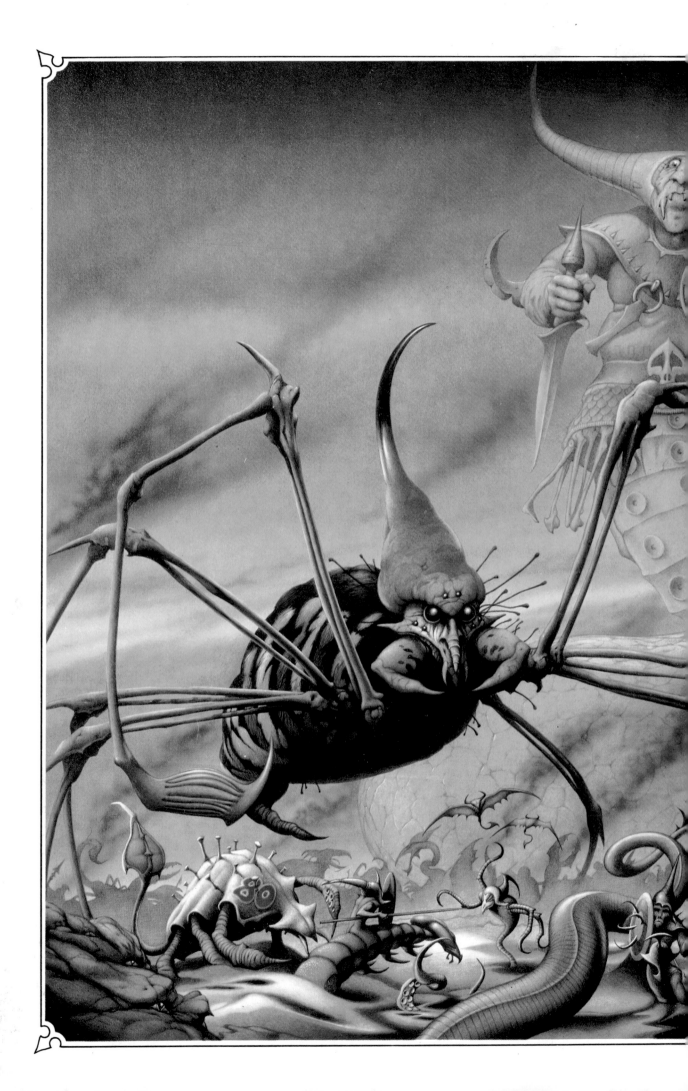

'6'

In Which Elric of Melniboné Resists the Temptations of the Chaos Lords

Elric reflected on the subtle way in which laughing Lords of Chaos had captured him. Apparently, he was merely a guest and quite free to wander where he would in their Realm. Actually, he was in their power as much as if they had chained him, for he could not flee this flying dragon and they had already demonstrated their enormous magical gifts in subtle ways, primarily with their shapechanging. Only the one who called himself Werther de Goethe (plainly a leader in the hierarchy of Chaos) still had the face and clothing he had worn when first encountered.

It was evident that this realm obeyed no natural laws, that it was mutable according to the whims of its powerful inhabitants. They could destroy him with a breath and had, subtly enough, given him evidence of that fact. How could he possibly escape such danger? By calling upon the Lords of Law for aid? But he owed them no loyalty and they, doubtless, regarded him as their enemy. But if he were to transfer his allegiance to Law . . .

These thoughts and more continued to engage him, while his captors chatted easily in the ancient High Speech of Melniboné, itself a version of the very language of Chaos. It was one of the other ways in which they revealed themselves for what they were. He fingered his runesword, wondering if it would be possible to slay such a lord and steal his energy, giving himself enough power for a little while to hurl himself back to his own sphere . . .

The one called Lord Werther was leaning over the side of the beast-vessel. 'Oh, come and see, Elric. Look!'

Reluctantly, the albino moved to where

Werther peered and pointed.

The entire landscape was filled with a monstrous battle. Creatures of all kinds and all combinations tore at one another with huge teeth and claws. Shapeless things slithered and hopped; giants, naked but for helmets and greaves, slashed at these beasts with great broadswords and axes, but were borne down. Flame and black smoke drifted everywhere. There was a smell. The stink of blood?

'What do you miss most?' asked the female. She pressed a soft body against him. He pretended not to be aware of it. He knew what magic flesh could hide on a she-witch.
'I miss peace,' said Elric almost to himself, 'and I miss war. For in battle I find a kind of peace . . .'

'Very good!' Bishop Castle applauded. 'You are beginning to learn our ways. You will soon become one of our best conversationalists.'

Elric touched the hilt of Stormbringer, hoping to feel it grow warm and vibrant under his hand, but it was still, impotent in the Realm

of Chaos. He uttered a heavy sigh.

'You are an adventurer, then, in your own world?' said the Duke of Queens. He was bluff. He had changed his beard to an ordinary sort of black and was wearing a scarlet costume; quilted doublet and tight-fitting hose, with a blue and white ruff, an elaborately feathered hat on his head. 'I, too, am something of a vagabond. As far, of course, as it is possible to be here. A buccaneer, of sorts. That is, my actions are in the main bolder than those of my fellows. More spectacular. Vulgar. Like yourself, sir. I admire your costume.'

Elric knew that this Duke of Hell was referring to the fact that he affected the costume of the southern barbarian, that he did not wear the more restrained colours and more cleverly wrought silks and metals of his own folk. He gave tit for tat at this time. He bowed.

'Thank you, sir. Your own clothes rival mine.'

'Do you think so?' The hell-lord pretended pleasure. If Elric had not known better, the creature would seem to be swelling with pride.

'Look!' cried Werther again. 'Look, Lord

Elric — we are attacked.'

Elric whirled.

From below were rising oddly-wrought vessels — something like ships, but with huge round wheels at their sides, like the wheels of water-clocks he had seen once in Pikarayd. Coloured smoke issued from chimneys mounted on their decks which swarmed with huge birds dressed in human clothing. The birds had multi-coloured plumage, curved beaks, and they held swords in their claws, while on their heads were strangely shaped black hats on which were blazed skulls with crossed bones beneath.

'Heave to!' squawked the birds. 'Or we'll put a shot across your bowels!'

'What can they be?' cried Biship Castle.

'Parrots,' said Werther de Goethe soberly. 'Otherwise known as the hawks of the sea. And they mean us no good.'

Mistress Christia blinked.

'Don't you mean pirates, dear?'

Elric took a firm grip on his sword. Some of the words the Chaos Lords used were absolutely meaningless to him. But whether the attacking creatures were of their own conception, or whether they were true enemies of his captors, Elric prepared to do bloody battle. His spirits improved. At least here was something substantial to fight.

In Which Mrs Persson Becomes Anxious About the Future of the Universe

Lord Jagged of Canaria was nowhere to be found. His huge castle, of gold and yellow spires, an embellished replica of Kings Cross station, was populated entirely by his quaint robots, whom Jagged found at once more mysterious and more trustworthy than android or human servants, for they could answer only according to a limited programme.

Una suspected that Jagged was, himself, upon some mission, for he, too, was a member of the League of Temporal Adventures. But she needed aid. Somehow she had to return Elric to his own dimensions without creating further disruptions in the fabric of Time and Space. The Conjunction was not due yet and, if things got any worse, might never come. So many plans depended on the Conjunction of the Million Spheres that she could not risk its failure. But she could not reveal too much either to Elric or his hosts. As a Guild member she was sworn to the utmost and indeed necessary secrecy. Even here at the End of

Time there were certain laws which could be disobeyed only at enormous risk. Words alone were dangerous when they described ideas concerning the nature of Time.

She racked her brains. She considered seeking out Jherek Carnelian, but then remembered that he had scarcely begun to understand his own destiny. Besides, there were certain similarities between Jherek and Elric which she could only sense at present. It would be best to go cautiously there.

She decided that she had no choice. She must return to the Time Centre and see if they could detect Lord Jagged for her.

She brought the necessary co-ordinates together in her mind and concentrated. For a moment all memories, all sense of identity left her.

Sergeant Alvarez was beside himself. His screens were no longer completely without form. Instead, peculiar shapes could be seen in the arrangements of lines. Una thought she saw faces, beasts, landscapes. That had never occurred before. The instruments, at least, had remained sane, even as they recorded insanity.

'It's getting worse,' said Alvarez. 'You've hardly any Time left. What there is, I've managed to borrow for you. Did you contact the rogue?'

She nodded. 'Yes. But getting him to return ... I want you to find Jagged.'

'Jagged? Are you sure?'

'It's our only chance, I think.'

Alvarez sighed and bent a tense back over his controls.

In Which Elric and Werther Fight Side by Side Against Almost Overwhelming Odds

Somewhere, it seemed to Elric, as he parried and thrust at the attacking bird-monsters, rich and rousing music played. It must be a delusion, brought on by battle-madness. Blood and feathers covered the carriage. He saw the one called Christia carried off screaming. Bishop Castle had disappeared. Gaf had gone. Only the three of them, shoulder to shoulder, continued to fight. What was disconcerting to Elric was that Werther and the Duke of Queens bore swords absolutely identical to Stormbringer. Perhaps they were the legendary Brothers of the Black Sword, said to reside in Chaos?

He was forced to admit to himself that he experienced a sense of comradeship with these two, who were braver than most in defending themselves against such dreadful, unlikely monsters — perhaps some creation of their own which had turned against them.

Having captured the Lady Christia, the birds began to return to their own craft.

'We must rescue her!' cried Werther as the flying ships began to retreat. 'Quickly! In pursuit!'

'Should we not seek reinforcements?' asked Elric, further impressed by the courage of this Chaos Lord.

'No time!' cried the Duke of Queens. 'After them!'

Werther shouted to his vessel. 'Follow those ships!'

The vessel did not move.

'It has an enchantment on it,' said Werther. 'We are stranded! Ah, and I loved her so much!'

Elric became suspicious again. Werther had

shown no signs, previously, of any affection for the female.

'You loved her?'

'From a distance,' Werther explained. 'Duke of Queens, what can we do? Those parrots will ransom her savagely and mishandle her objects of virtue!'

'Dastardly poltroons!' roared the huge duke.

Elric could make little sense of this exchange. It dawned on him, then, that he could still hear the rousing music. He looked below. On some sort of dais in the middle of the bizarre landscape a large group of musicians was assembled. They played on, apparently oblivious of what happened above. This was truly a world dominated by Chaos.

Their ship began slowly to fall towards the band. It lurched. Elric gasped and clung to the side as they struck yielding ground and bumped to a halt.

The Duke of Queens, apparently elated, was already scrambling overboard. 'There! We can follow on those mounts.'

Tethered near the dais was a herd of

creatures bearing some slight resemblance to horses but in a variety of dazzling, metallic colours, with horns and bony ridges on their backs. Saddles and bridles of alien workmanship showed that they were domestic beasts, doubtless belonging to the musicians.

'They will want some payment from us, surely,' said Elric, as they hurried towards the horses.

'Ah, true!' Werther reached into a purse at his belt and drew forth a handful of jewels. Casually he flung them towards the musicians and climbed into the saddle of the nearest beast. Elric and the Duke of Queens followed his example. Then Werther, with a whoop, was off in the direction in which the bird-monsters had gone.

The landscape of this world of Chaos changed rapidly as they rode. They galloped through forests of crystalline trees, over fields of glowing flowers, leapt rivers the colour of blood and the consistency of mercury, and their tireless mounts maintained a headlong pace which never faltered. Through clouds of boiling gas which wept, through rain, through

snow, through intolerable heat, through shallow lakes in which oddly fashioned fish wriggled and gasped, until at last a range of mountains came in sight.

'There!' panted Werther, pointing with his own rune-sword. 'Their lair. Oh, the fiends! How can we climb such smooth cliffs?'

It was true that the base of the cliffs rose some hundred feet before they became suddenly ragged, like the rotting teeth of the beggars of Nadsokor. They were of dusky, purple obsidian and so smooth as to reflect the faces of the three adventurers who stared at them in despair.

It was Elric who saw the steps put into the side of the cliff.

These will take us up some of the way, at least.'

'It could be a trap,' said the Duke of Queens. He, too, seemed to be relishing the opportunity to take action. Although a Lord of Chaos there was something about him that made Elric respond to a fellow spirit.

'Let them trap us,' said Elric laconically. 'We have our swords.'

With a wild laugh, Werther de Goethe was the first to swing himself from his saddle and run towards the steps, leaping up them almost as if he had the power of flight. Elric and the Duke of Queens followed more slowly.

Their feet slipping in the narrow spaces not meant for mortals to climb, ever aware of the dizzying drop on their left, the three came at last to the top of the cliff and stood clinging to sharp crags, staring across a plain at a crazy castle rising into the clouds before them.

'Their stronghold,' said Werther.

'What are these creatures?' Elric asked. 'Why do they attack you? Why do they capture the Lady Christia?'

'They nurse an abiding hatred for us,' explained the Duke of Queens, and looked expectantly at Werther, who added:

'This was their world before it became ours.'

'And before it became theirs,' said the Duke of Queens, 'it was the world of the Yargtroon.'

'The Yargtroon?' Elric frowned.

'They dispossessed the bodiless vampire goat-folk of Kia,' explained Werther. 'Who, in turn, destroyed — or thought they destroyed

— the Grash-Tu-Xem, a race of Old Ones older than any Old Ones except the Elder Old Ones of Ancient Thriss.'

'Older even than Chaos?' asked Elric.

'Oh, far older,' said Werther.

'It's almost completely collapsed, it's so old,' added the Duke of Queens.

Elric was baffled. 'Thriss?'

'Chaos,' said the duke.

Elric let a thin smile play about his lips. 'You still mock me, my lord. The power of Chaos is the greatest there is, only equalled by the power of Law.'

'Oh, certainly,' agreed the Duke of Queens.

Elric became suspicious again. 'Do you play with me, my lord?'

'Well, naturally, we try to please our guests …'

Werther interrupted. 'Yonder doomy edifice holds the one I love. Somewhere within its walls she is incarcerated, while ghouls taunt at her and devils threaten.'

'The bird-monsters …?' began Elric.

'Chimerae,' said the Duke of Queens. 'You saw only one of the shapes they assume.'

Elric understood this. 'Aha!'

'But how can we enter it?' Werther spoke almost to himself.

'We must wait until nightfall,' said Elric, 'and enter under the cover of darkness.'

'Nightfall?' Werther brightened.

Suddenly they were in utter darkness.

Somewhere the Duke of Queens lost his footing and fell with a muffled curse.

In Which Mrs Persson At Last Makes Contact With Her Old Friend

They stood together beneath the striped awning of the tent while a short distance away armoured men, mounted on armoured horses, jousted, were injured or died. The two members wore appropriate costumes for the period. Lord Jagged looked handsome in his surcoat and mail, but Una Persson merely looked uncomfortable in her wimple and kirtle.

'I can't leave just now,' he was saying. 'I am laying the foundations for a very important development.'

'Which will come to nothing unless Elric is returned,' she said.

A knight with a broken lance thundered past, covering them in dust.

'Well played Sir Holger!' called Lord Jagged. 'An ancestor of mine, you know,' he told her.

'You will not be able to recognize the world of the End of Time when you return, if this is allowed to continue,' she said.

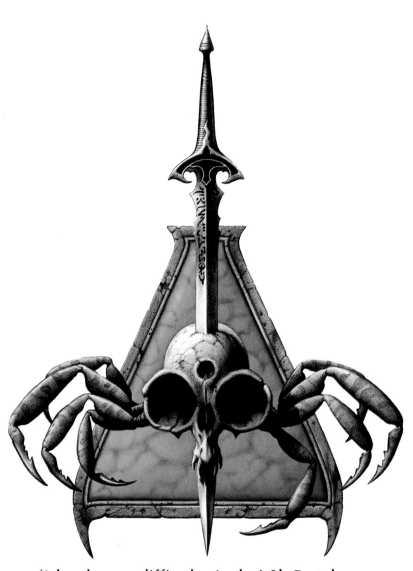

'It's always difficult, isn't it?' But he was listening to her now.

'These disruptions could as easily affect us and leave us stranded,' she added. 'We would lose any freedom we have gained.'

He bit into a pomegranate and offered it to

her. 'You can only get these in this area. Did you know? Impossible to find in England. In the thirteenth century, at any rate. The idea of freedom is such a nebulous one, isn't it? Most of the time when angry people are speaking of "freedom" what they are actually asking for is much simpler — respect. Do those in authority or those with power ever really respect those who do not have power?' He paused. 'Or do they mean "power" and not "freedom". Or are they the same ...?'

'Really, Jagged, this is no time for self-indulgence.'

He looked about him. 'There's little else to do in the Middle East in the thirteenth century, I assure you, except eat pomegranates and philosophize ...'

'You must come back to the End of Time'.

He wiped his handsome chin. 'Your urgency,' he said, 'worries me, Una. These matters should be handled with delicacy — slowly ...'

'The entire fabric will collapse unless he is returned to his own dimension. He is an important factor in the whole plan.'

'Well, yes, I understand that.'

'He is, in one sense at least, your protégé.'

'I know, But not my responsibility.'

'You must help,' she said.
There was a loud bang and a crash.
A splinter flew into Mrs Persson's eye.
'Oh, zounds!' she said.

In Which The Castle Is Assaulted And The Plot Thickened

A moon had appeared above the spires of the castle which seemed to Elric to have changed its shape since he had first seen it. He meant to ask his companions for an explanation, but at present they were all sworn to silence as they crept nearer. From within the castle burst light, emanating from guttering brands stuck into brackets on the walls. There was laughter, noise of feasting. Hidden behind a rock they peered through one large window and inspected the scene within.

The entire hall was full of men wearing identical costumes. They had black skull caps, loose white blouses and trousers, black shoes. Their eyebrows were black in dead white faces, even paler than Elric's and they had bright red lips.

'Aha', whispered Werther, 'the parrots are celebrating their victory. Soon they will be too drunk to know what is happening to them.'

'Parrots?' said Elric. 'What is that word?'

'Pierrots, he means,' said the Duke of

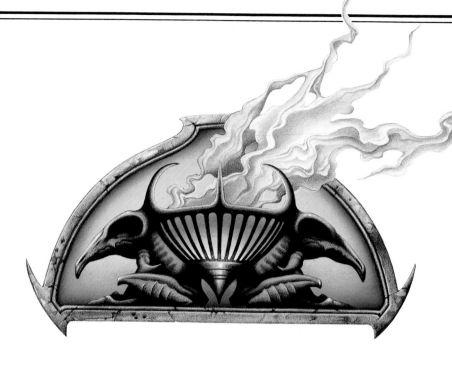

Queens. 'Don't you, Werther?' There were evidently certain words which did not translate easily into the High Speech of Melniboné.

'Sshh,' said the Last Romantic, 'they will capture us and torture us to death if they detect our presence.'

They worked their way around the castle. It was guarded at intervals by gigantic warriors whom Elric at first mistook for statues, save that, when he looked closely, he could see them breathing very slowly. They were un-armed, but their fists and feet were dis-proportionately large and could crush any intruder they detected.

'They are sluggish, by the look of them,' said Elric, 'If we are quick, we can run beneath them and enter the castle before they realize it. Let me try first. If I succeed, you follow.'

Werther clapped his new comrade on the back. 'Very well.'

Elric waited until the nearest guard halted and spread his huge feet apart, then he dashed forward, scuttling like an insect between the giant's legs and flinging himself through a dimly lit window. He found himself in some sort of store-room. He had not been seen, though the guard cocked his ear for half a moment before resuming his pace.

Elric looked cautiously out and signalled to his companions. The Duke of Queens waited for the guard to stop again, then he, too, made for the window and joined Elric. He was panting and grinning. 'This is wonderful,' he said.

Elric admired his spirit. There was no doubt that the guard could crush any of them to a pulp, even if (as still nagged at his brain) this was all some sort of complicated illusion.

Another dash, and Werther was with them.

Cautiously, Elric opened the door of the store-room. They looked onto a deserted landing. They crossed the landing and looked over a balustrade. They had expected to see another hall, but instead there was a miniature lake on which floated the most beautiful miniature ship, all mother-of-pearl, brass and ebony, with golden sails and silver masts. Surrounding this ship were mermaids and mermen bearing trays of exotic food (reminding Elric how hungry he still was) which they fed to the ship's only passenger, Mistress Christia.

'She is under an enchantment,' said Elric. 'They beguile her with illusions so that she will not wish to come with us even if we do rescue her. Do you know no counter-spells?'

Werther thought for a moment. Then he shook his head.

'You must be very minor Lords of Chaos,' said Elric, biting his lower lip.

From the lake, Mistress Christia giggled and drew one of the mermaids towards her. 'Come here, my pretty piscine!'

'Mistress Christia!' hissed Werther de Goethe.

'Oh!' The captive widened her eyes (which were now both large and blue). 'At last!'

'You wish to be rescued?' said Elric.

'Rescued? Only by you, most alluring of albinoes!'

Elric hardened his features. 'I am not the one who loves you, madam.'

'What? I am loved? By whom? By you, Duke of Queens?'

'Sshh,' said Elric. 'The demons will hear us.'

'Oh, of course,' said Mistress Christia gravely, and fell silent for a second. 'I'll get rid of all this, shall I?'

And she touched one of her rings.

Ship, lake and merfolk were gone. She lay on silken cushions, attended by monkeys.

'Sorcery!' said Elric, 'If she has such power, then why —?'

'It is limited,' explained Werther. 'Merely to such tricks.'

'Quite,' said Mistress Christia.

Elric glared at them. 'You surrounded me with illusions. You make me think I am aiding you, when really . . .'

'No, no!' cried Werther. 'I assure you, Lord Elric, you have our greatest respect — well, mine at least — we are only attempting to —'

There was a roar from the gallery above.

Rank upon rank of grinning demons looked down upon them. They were armed to the teeth.

'Hurry!' The Duke of Queens leapt to the cushions and seized Mistress Christia, flinging her over his shoulder. 'We can never defeat so many!'

The demons were already rushing down the circular staircase. Elric, still not certain whether his new friends deceived him or not, made a decision. He called to the Duke of Queens. 'Get her from the castle. We'll keep them from you for a few moments, at least.' He could not help himself. He behaved impulsively.

The Duke of Queens, sword in hand, Mistress Christia over the other shoulder, ran into a narrow passage. Elric and Werther stood together as the demons rushed down on them. Blade met blade. There was an unbearable shrilling of steel mingled with the cacklings and shrieks of the demons as they gnashed their teeth and rolled their eyes and slashed at the pair with swords, knives and axes. But worst of all was the smell. The dreadful smell of burning flesh which filled the air and

threatened to choke Elric. It came from the demons. The smell of Hell. He did his best to cover his nostrils as he fought, certain that the smell must overwhelm him before the swords. Above him was a set of metal rungs fixed into the stones, leading high into a kind of chimney. As a pause came he pointed upward to Werther, who understood him. For a moment they managed to drive the demons back. Werther jumped onto Elric's shoulders (again displaying a strange lightness) and reached down to haul the albino after him.

While the demons wailed and cackled below, they began to climb the chimney.

They climbed for nearly fifty feet before they found themselves in a small, round room whose windows looked out over the purple crags and, beyond them, to a scene of bleak rocky pavements pitted with holes, like some vast unlikely cheese.

And there, rolling over this relatively flat landscape, in full daylight (for the sun had risen) was the Duke of Queens in a carriage of brass and wood, studded with jewels, and drawn by two bovine creatures which looked to Elric as if they might be the fabulous oxen of mythology who had drawn the war-chariot of his ancestors to do battle with the emerging nations of mankind.

Mistress Christia was beside the Duke of Queens. They seemed to be waiting for Elric and Werther.

'It's impossible,' said the albino. 'We could not get out of this tower, let alone those crags. I wonder how they managed to move so quickly and so far. And where did the chariot itself come from?'

'Stolen, no doubt, from the demons,' said Werther. 'See, there are wings here.' He indicated a heap of feathers in the corner of the room. 'We can use those.'

'What wizardry is this?' said Elric. 'Man cannot fly on bird wings.'

'With the appropriate spell he can,' said Werther. 'I am not that well versed in the magic arts, of course, but let me see ...' He picked up one set of wings. They were soft and glinted with subtle, rainbow colours. He placed them on Elric's back, murmuring his spell:

Oh, for the wings, for the wings of a dove,
To carry me to the one I love . . .

'There!' He was very pleased with himself. Elric moved his shoulders and his wings began to flap. 'Excellent! Off you go, Elric. I'll join you in a moment.'

Elric hesitated, then saw the head of the first demon emerging from the hole in the floor. He jumped to the window ledge and leapt into space. The wings sustained him. Against all logic he flew smoothly towards the waiting chariot and behind him, came Werther de Goethe. At the windows of the tower the demons crowded, shaking fists and weapons as their prey escaped them.

Elric landed rather awkwardly beside the chariot and was helped aboard by the Duke of Queens. Werther joined them, dropping expertly amongst them. He moved the wings from the albino's back and nodded to the Duke of Queens who yelled at the oxen, cracking his whip as they began to move.

Mistress Christia flung her arms about Elric's neck. 'What courage! What resourcefulness!' she breathed. 'Without you, I should now be ruined!'

Elrich sheathed Stormbringer. 'We all three worked together for your rescue, madam.' Gently he removed her arms. Courteously he bowed and leaned against the far side of the chariot as it bumped and hurtled over the peculiar rocky surface.

'Swifter! Swifter!' called the Duke of Queens, casting urgent looks backwards. 'We are followed!'

From the disappearing tower there now poured a host of flying, gibbering things. Once again the creatures had changed shape and had assumed the form of striped, winged cats, all glaring eyes, fangs and extended claws.

The rock became viscous, clogging the wheels of the chariot, as they reached what appeared to be a silvery road, flowing between the high trees of an alien forest already touched by a weird twilight.

The first of the flying cats caught up with them, slashing.

Elric drew Stormbringer and cut back. The beast roared in pain, blood streaming from its severed leg, its wings flapping in Elric's face as it hovered and attempted to snap at the sword.

The chariot rolled faster, through the forest to green fields touched by the moon. The days were short, it seemed, in this part of chaos. A path stretched skyward. The Duke of Queens drove the chariot straight up it, heading for the moon itself.

The moon grew larger and larger and still the demons pursued them, but they could not fly as fast as the chariot which went so swiftly that sorcery must surely speed it. Now they could only be heard in the darkness behind and the silver moon was huge.

'There!' called Werther. 'There is safety!'

On they raced until the moon was reached, the oxen leaping in their traces, galloping over the gleaming surface to where a white palace awaited them.

'Sanctuary,' said the Duke of Queens. And he laughed a wild, full laugh of sheer joy.

The palace was like ivory, carved and wrought by a million hands, every inch covered with delicate designs.

Elric wondered. 'Where is this place?' he asked. 'Does it lie outside the Realm of

Chaos?'

Werther seemed non-plussed. 'You mean our world?'

'Aye.'

'It is still part of our world,' said the Duke of Queens.

'Is the palace to your liking?' asked Werther.

'It is lovely.'

'A trifle pale for my own taste,' said the Last Romantic. 'It was Mistress Christia's idea.'

'You built this?' The albino turned to the woman. 'When?'

'Just now.' She seemed surprised.

Elric nodded. 'Aha. It is within the power of Chaos to create whatever whims it pleases.'

The chariot crossed a white drawbridge and entered a white courtyard. In it grew white flowers. They dismounted and entered a huge hall, white as bone, in which red lights glowed. Again Elric began to suspect mockery, but the faces of the Chaos lords showed only pleasure. He realized that he was dizzy with hunger and weariness, as he had been ever since he had been flung into this terrible world where no shape was constant, no idea permanent.

'Are you hungry?' asked Mistress Christia.

He nodded. And suddenly the room was filled by a long table on which all kinds of food were heaped — and everything, meats and fruits and vegetables, was white.

Elric moved to take the seat she indicated and he put some of the food on a silver plate and he touched it to his lips and he tasted it. It was delicious. Forgetting suspicion, he began to eat heartily, trying not to consider the colourless quality of the meal. Werther and the Duke of Queens also took some food, but it seemed they ate only from politeness. Werther glanced up at the faraway roof. 'What a wonderful tomb this would make,' he said. 'Your imagination improves, Mistress Christia.'

'Is this your domain?' asked Elric. 'The moon?'

'Oh no,' she said. 'It was all made for the occasion.'

'Occasion?'

'For your adventure,' she said. Then she fell silent.

Elric became grave. 'Those demons? They were not your enemies. They belong to you!'

'Belong?' said Mistress Christia. She shook her head.

Elric frowned and pushed back his plate. 'I am, however, most certainly your captive.' He stood up and paced the white floor. 'Will you not return me to my own plane?'

'You would come back almost immediately, said Werther de Goethe. 'It is called the Morphail Effect. And if you did not come here, you would yet remain in your own future. It is in the nature of Time.'

'This is nonsense,' said Elric. 'I have left my own realm before and returned — though admittedly memory becomes weak, as with dreams poorly recalled.'

'No man can go back in Time,' said the Duke of Queens. 'Ask Brannart Morphail.'

'He, too, is a Lord of Chaos?'

'If you like. He is a colleague.'

'Could he not return me to my realm? He sounds a clever being.'

'He could not and he would not,' said Mistress Christia. 'Haven't you enjoyed your experiences here so far?'

'Enjoyed?' Elric was astonished. 'Madam, I think ... Well, what has happened this day is

not what we mortals would call "enjoyment"!'

'But you *seemed* to be enjoying yourself,' said the Duke of Queens in some disappointment. 'Didn't he, Werther?'

'You were much more cheerful through the whole episode,' agreed the Last Romantic. 'Particularly when you were fighting the demons.'

'As with many time-travellers who suffer from anxieties,' said Mistress Christia, 'you appeared to relax when you had something immediate to capture your attention ...'

Elric refused to listen. This was clever Chaos talk, meant to deceive him and take his mind from his chief concern.

'If I was any help to you,' he began, 'I am, of course ...'

'He isn't very grateful,' Mistress Christia pouted.

Elric felt madness creeping nearer again. He calmed himself.

'I thank you for the food, madam. Now, I would sleep.'

'Sleep?' she was disconcerted. 'Oh! Of course. Yes. A bedroom?'

'If you have such a thing.'

'As many as you like.' She moved a stone on one of her rings. The walls seemed to draw back to show bedchamber after bedchamber, in all manner of styles, with beds of every shape and fashion. Elric controlled his temper. He bowed, thanked her, said goodnight to the two lords and made for the nearest bed.

As he closed the door behind him, he thought he heard Werther de Goether say: 'We must try to think of a better entertainment for him when he wakes up.'

'W'

In Which Mrs Persson Witnesses The First Sign Of The Megaflow's Disintegration

In Castle Canaria Lord Jagged unrolled his antique charts. He had had them drawn for him by a baffled astrologer in 1950. They were one of his many affectations. At the moment, however, they were of considerably greater use than Alvarez's electronics.

While he used a wrist computer to check his figures, Una Persson looked out of the window of Castle Canaria and wondered who had invented this particular landscape. A green and orange sum cast sickening light over the herds of grazing beasts who resembled, from this distance at any rate, nothing so much as gigantic human hands. In the middle of the scene was raised some kind of building in the shape of a vast helmet, vaguely Greek in conception. Beyond that was a low, grey moon. She turned away.

'I must admit,' said Lord Jagged, 'that I had not understood the extent . . .'

'Exactly,' she said.

'You must forgive me. A certain amount of

amnesia — euphoria, perhaps? — always comes over one in these very remote periods.'

'Quite'.

He looked up from the charts. 'We've a few hours at most.'

Her smile was thin, her nod barely perceptible.

While she made the most of having told him so, Lord Jagged frowned, turned a power ring and produced an already lit pipe which he placed thoughtfully in his mouth, taking it out again almost immediately. 'That wan't Dunhill Standard Medium.' He laid the pipe aside.

There came a loud buzzing noise from the window. The scene outside was disintegrating as if melting on glass. An eerie golden light spread everywhere, flooding from an apex of deeper gold, as if forming a funnel.

'That's a rupture,' said Lord Jagged. His voice was tense. He put his arm about her shoulders. 'I've never seen anything of the size before.'

Rushing towards them along the funnel of light there came an entire city of turrets and towers and minarets in a wide variety of pastel colours. It was set into a saucer-shaped base which was almost certainly several miles in circumference.

For a moment the city seemed to retreat. The golden light faded. The city remained, some distance away, swaying a little as if on a gentle tide, a couple of thousand feet above the ground, the grey moon below it.

'That's what I call megaflow distortion,' said Una Persson in that inappropriately facetious tone adopted by those who are deeply frightened.

'I recognize the period.' Jagged drew a telescope from his robes. 'Second Candlemaker's Empire, mainly based in Arcturus. This is a village by their standards. After all, Earth was merely a rural park during that time.' He retreated into academe, his own response to fear.

Una craned her head. 'Isn't that some sort of vehicle heading towards the city. From the moon — good heavens, they've spotted it already. Are they going to try to put the whole thing into a menagerie?'

Jagged had the advantage of the telescope. 'I think not.' He handed her the instrument.

Through it she saw a scarlet and black chariot borne by what seemed to be some form of flying fairground horses. In the chariot, armed to the teeth with lances, bows, spears, swords, axes, morningstars, maces and almost every other barbaric hand-weapon, clad in quasi-mythological armour, were Werther de Goethe, the Duke of Queens and Elric of Meniborné.

'They're attacking it!' she said faintly. 'What will happen when the two groups intersect?'

'Three groups,' he pointed out. 'Untangling that in a few hours is going to be even harder.'

'And if we fail?'

He shrugged. 'We might just as well give ourselves up to the biggest chronoquake the universe has ever experienced.'

'You're exaggerating,' she said.

'Why not? Everyone else is.'

'12'

The Attack On The Citadel Of The Skies

'Melniboné! Melniboné!' cried the albino as the chariot circled over the spires and turrets of the city. They saw startled faces below. Strange engines were being dragged through the narrow streets.

'Surrender!' Elric demanded.

'I do not think they can understand us,' said the Duke of Queens. 'What a find, eh? A whole city from the past!'

Werther had been reluctant to embark on an adventure not of his own creation, but Elric, realizing that here at last was a chance of escape, had been anxious to begin. The Duke of Queens had, in an instant, aided the albino by producing costumes, weapons, transport. Within minutes of the city's appearance, they had been on their way.

Exactly why Elric wished to attack the city, Werther could not make out, unless it was some test of the Melnibonéan's to see if his companions were true allies or merely pretending to have befriended him. Werther was learning a great deal from Elric, much more than he had ever learned from Mongrove, whose ideas of angst were only marginally less notional than Werther's own.

A broad, flat blue ray beamed from the city. It singed one wheel of the chariot.

'Ha! They make sorcerous weapons,' said Elric. 'Well, my friends. Let us see you counter with your own power.'

Werther obediently imitated the blue ray and sent it back from his fingers, slicing the tops off several towers. The Duke of Queens typically let loose a different coloured ray from each of his extended ten fingers and bored a hole all the way through the bottom of the city so that fields could be seen below. He was pleased with the effect.

'This is the power of the Gods of Chaos!' cried Elric, a familiar elation filling him as the blood of old Melniboné was fired. 'Surrender!'

'Why do you want them to surrender?' asked the Duke of Queens in some disappointment.

'Their city evidently has the power to fly through the dimensions. If I became its lord I could force it to return to my own plane,' said

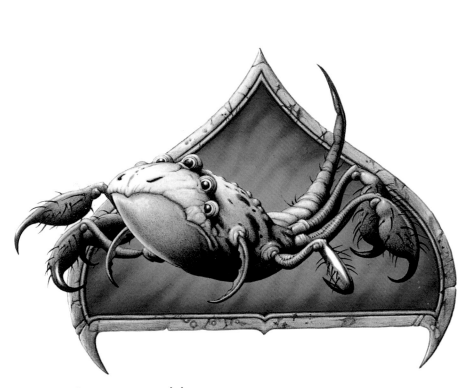

Elric reasonably.

'The Morphail Effect . . .' began Werther, but realized he was spoiling the spirit of the game. 'Sorry'.

The blue ray came again, but puttered out and faded before it reached them.

'Their power is gone!' cried Elric. 'Your sorcery defeats them, my lords. Let us land and demand they honour us as their new rulers.'

With a sigh, Werther ordered the chariot to set down in the largest square. Here they waited until a few of the citizens began to arrive, cautious and angry, but evidently in no mood to give any further resistance.

Elric addressed them. 'It was necessary to attack and conquer you, for I must return to my own Realm, there to fulfil my great destiny. If you will take me to Melniboné, I will demand nothing further from you.'

'One of us really ought to take a translation pill,' said Werther. 'These people probably have no idea where they are.'

A meaningless babble came from the citizens. Elric frowned. 'They understand not the High Speech,' he said. 'I will try the Common Tongue.' He spoke in a language neither Werther, the Duke of Queens nor the citizens of this settlement could understand.

He began to show signs of frustration. He drew his sword Stormbringer. 'By the Black Sword, know that I am Elric, last of the royal line of Melniboné! You must obey me. Is there none here who understands the High Speech?'

Then, from the crow, stepped a being far taller than the others. He was dressed in robes of dark blue and deepest scarlet and his face was haughty, beautiful and full of evil.

'I speak the High Tongue,' he said.

Werther and the Duke of Queens were non-plussed. This was no one they recognized.

Elric gestured. 'You are the ruler of city?'

'Call me that, if you will.'

'Your name?'

'I am known by many names. And you know me, Elric of Melniboné, for I am your lord and your friend.'

'Ah', said Elric lowering his sword, 'this is the greatest deception of them all. I am a fool.'

'Merely a mortal,' said the newcomer, his voice soft, amused and full of a subtle arrogance. 'Are these the renegades who helped you?'

'Renegades?' said Werther. 'Who are you, sir?'

'You should know me, rogue lords. You aid a mortal and defy your brothers of Chaos.'

'Eh?' said the Duke of Queens. 'I haven't got a brother.'

The stranger ignored him. 'Demigods who thought that by helping this mortal they could threaten the power of the Greater Ones.'

'So you did aid me against your own,' said

Elric. 'Oh, my friends!'

'And they shall be punished!'

Werther began: 'We regret any damage to your city. After all, you were not invited . . .'

The Duke of Queens was laughing. 'Who are you? What disguise is this?'

'Know me for your master.' The eyes of the stranger glowed with myriad fires. 'Know me for Arioch, Duke of Hell!'

'Arioch!' Elric became filled with a strange joy. 'Arioch! I called upon thee and was not answered!'

'I was not in this Realm,' said the Duke of Hell. 'I was forced to be absent. And while I was gone, fools thought to displace me.'

'I really cannot follow all this,' said the Duke of Queens. He set aside his mace. 'I must confess I become a trifle bored, sir. If you will excuse me.'

'You will not escape me.' Arioch lifted a languid hand and the Duke of Queens was frozen to the ground, unable to move anything save his eyes.

'You are interfering, sir, with a perfectly —' Werther too was struck dumb and paralysed.

But Elric refused to quail. 'Lord Arioch, I have given you blood and souls. You owe me . . .'

'I owe you nothing, Elric of Melniborné. Nothing I do not choose to owe. You are my slave . . .'

'No,' said Elric. 'I serve you. There are old bonds. But you cannot control me, Lord Arioch, for I have a power within me which you fear. It is the power of my very mortality.'

The Duke of Hell shrugged. 'You will remain in the Realm of Chaos forever. Your mortality will avail you little here.'

'You need me in my own Realm, to be your agent. That, too, I know, Lord Arioch.'

The handsome head lowered a fraction as if Arioch considered this. The beautiful lips smiled. 'Aye, Elric. It is true that I need you to do my work. For the moment it is impossible for the Lord of Chaos to interfere directly in the world of mortals, for we should threaten our own existence. The rate of entropy would increase beyond even our control. The day has not yet come when Law and Chaos must decide the issue once and for all. But it will come soon enough for you, Elric.'

'And my sword will be at your service, Lord Arioch.'

'Will it Elric?'

Elric was surprised by this doubting tone. He had always served Chaos, as his ancestors had. 'Why should I turn against you? Law has no attractions for one such as Elric of Melniborné.'

The Duke of Hell was silent.

'And there is the bargain,' added Elric. 'Return me to my own Realm, Lord Arioch, so that I might keep it.'

Arioch sighed. 'I am reluctant.' 'I demand it,' bravely said the albino.

'Oho!' Arioch was amused. 'Well, mortal, I'll reward your courage and I'll punish your insolence. The reward will be that you are returned from whence you came, before you called on Chaos in your battle with that pathetic wizard. The punishment is that you will recall every incident that occurred since then — but only in your dreams. You will be haunted by the puzzle for the rest of your life — and you will never for a moment be able to express what mystifies you.'

Elric smiled. 'I am already haunted by a curse of that kind, my lord.'

'Be that as it may, I have made my decision.

'I accept it,' said the albino, and he sheathed his sword, Stormbringer.

'Then come with me,' said Arioch, Duke of Hell. And he drifted forward, took Elric by the arm, and lifted them both high into the sky, floating over distorted scenes, half-formed dream-worlds, the whims of the Lords of Chaos, until they came to a gigantic rock shaped like a skull. And through one of the eye-sockets Lord Arioch bore Elric of Melni-borné. And down strange corridors that whispered and displayed all manner of treasures. And up into a landscape, a desert in which grew many strange plants, while overhead could be seen a land of snow and mountains, equally alien. And from his robes Arioch, Duke of Hell produced a wand and he bade Elric to take hold of the wand, which was hot to the touch and glittered, and he placed his own slender hand at the other end, and he murmured words which Elric could not understand and together they began to fade from the landscape, into the darkness of limbo where many eyes accused them, to an island in a grey and storm-tossed sea; an island littered with destruction and with the dead.

Then Arioch, Duke of Hell, laughed a little and vanished, leaving the Prince of Melniboné sprawled amongst corpses and ruins while heavy rain beat down upon him.

And in the scabbard at Elric's side, Stormbringer stirred and murmured once more.

13

In Which There Is A Small Celebration At The End Of Time

Werther de Goethe and the Duke of Queens blinked their eyes and found that they could move their heads. They stood in a large, pleasant room full of charts and ancient instruments. Mistress Christia was there, too.

Una Persson was smiling as she watched golden light fade from the sky. The city had disappeared, hardly any the worse for its experience. She had managed to save the two friends without a great deal of fuss, for the citizens had still been bewildered by what had happened to them. Because of the megaflow distortion, the Morphail Effect would not manifest itself. They would never understand where they had been or what had actually happened.

'Who on earth was that fellow who turned up?' asked the Duke of Queens. 'Some friend of yours, Mrs Persson? He's certainly no sportsman.'

'Oh, I wouldn't agree. You could call him

the ultimate sportsman,' she said. 'I am acquainted with him, as a matter of fact.'

'It's not Jagged in disguise is it?' said Mistress Christia who did not really know what had gone on. 'This is Jagged's castle — but where is Jagged?'

'You are aware how mysterious he is,' Una answered. 'I happened to be here when I saw that Werther and the Duke were in trouble in the city and was able to be of help.'

Werther scowled (a very good copy of Elric's own scowl). 'Well, it isn't good enough.'

'It was a jolly adventure while it lasted, you must admit,' said the Duke of Queens.

'It wasn't meant to be jolly,' said Werther. 'It was meant to be significant.'

Lord Jagged entered the room. He wore his familiar yellow robes. 'How pleasant,' he said. 'When did all of you arrive?'

'I have been here for some time,' Mrs Persson explained, 'but Werther and the Duke of Queens . . .'

'Just got here,' explained the Duke. 'I hope we're not intruding. Only we had a slight mishap and Mrs Persson was good enough . . .'

'Always delighted,' said the insincere lord. 'Would you care to see my new — ?'

'I'm on my way home,' said the Duke of Queens. 'I just stopped by. Mrs Persson will explain.'

'I, too,' said Werther suspiciously, 'am on my way back.'

'Very well. Goodbye.'

Wether summoned an aircar, a restrained figure of death, in rags with a sickle, who picked the three up in his hand and bore them towards a bleak horizon.

It was only days later, when he went to visit Mongrove to tell him of his adventures and solicit his friend's advice, that Werther realized he was still speaking High Melnibonéan. Some nagging thought remained with him for a long while after that. It concerned Lord Jagged, but he could not quite work out what was involved.

After this incident there were no further disruptions at the End of Time until the beginning of the story concerning Jherek Carnelian and Miss Amelia Underwood.

˙14˙

**In Which Elric of Melniboné Recovers
From a Variety of Enchantments and Becomes
Determined to Return to the Dreaming City**

Elric was awakened by the rain on his face. Wearily he peered around him. To left and right there were only the dismembered corpses of the dead, the Krettii and the Fikharian sailors destroyed during his battle with the half-brute who had somehow gained so much sorcerous power. He shook his milk-white hair and he raised crimson eyes to the grey, boiling sky.

It seemed that Arioch had aided him, after all. The sorcerer was destroyed and he, Elric, remained alive. He recalled the sweet, bantering tones of his patron demon. Familiar tones, yet he could not remember what the words had been.

He dragged himself over the dead and waded through the shallows towards the Filkharian ship which still had some of its crew. They were, by now, anxious to head out into open sea again rather than face any more terrors on Sorcerer's Isle.

He was determined to see Cymoril, whom he loved, to regain his throne from Yyrkoon, his cousin . . .

15

In Which A Brief Reunion Takes Place At the Time Centre

With the manuscript of Colonel Pyat's rather dangerous volume of memoirs safely back in her briefcase, Una Persson decided it was the right moment to check into the Time Centre. Alvarez should be on duty again and his instruments should be registering any minor imbalances resulting from the episode concerning the gloomy albino.

Alvarez was not alone. Lord Jagged was there, in a disreputable Norfolk jacket and smoking a battered briar. He had evidently been holidaying in Victorian England. He was pleased to see her.

Alvarez ran his gear through all functions. 'Sweet and neat,' he said. 'It hasn't been as good since I don't know when. We've you to thank for that, Mrs P.'

She was modest.

'Certainly not. Jagged was the one. Your disguise was wonderful, Jagged. How did you manage to imitate that character so thoroughly? It convinced Elric. He really thought you were whatever it was — a Chaos Duke?'

Jagged waved a modest hand.

'I mean,' said Una, 'it's almost as if you *were* this fellow "Arioch" . . .'

But Lord Jagged only puffed on his pipe and smiled a secret and superior smile.

THE END